P9-DGE-240

Trying

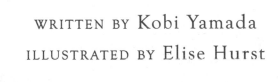

WRITTEN BY Kobi Yamada

ILLUSTRATED BY Elise Hurst

"How do you do that?"

I didn't realize I had said it out loud,
but the sculptor looked over and replied,
"You simply do it."

"Oh no, I could never do that."

"How do you know?" he asked.

"I just know."

Confused, I walked away. "He must be joking," I thought.

But as I left, I couldn't help wondering what it would be like
to create something so incredible.

When I returned, the sculptor looked over at me
and asked, "How is your sculpture coming along?"

"I'm just here to watch."

"The best way to give your talents an opportunity
is to try," he responded.

"I'd rather just watch. I can't mess things up
if I just watch."

"Ah, yes." He nodded. "If you do nothing,
it feels safe, but everything stays the same.
If you do nothing, there is less to experience,
less to love, and less to learn.

"The fear of failing is the scariest part, and it stops most people from starting. The only way to get to where you want to go is to take a step in that direction.

"And the best way to do that is to begin."

It was all I could think about.

Even as I slept, I dreamt of creating beautiful things.

I was excited to get started.

But as I was working, I realized that something was wrong.
With every strike, I felt a little more deflated. With every blow,
my disappointment grew. This was not turning out the way I had imagined.

Why did I think I could do it? Why had I let myself care about this so much?

The next time I saw the sculptor, he asked about my work.
I told him it was no good and that I had quit.

"Why would you do that?" he asked.

"Because it feels awful to want something so badly, and then
just be disappointed."

"Yes," the sculptor replied, "disappointment hurts. But failure
is temporary, and in many ways, necessary. It shows us how
something can't be done, which means we are a little closer to
finding out how it can.

"When you first tried to walk, you fell. But you picked yourself up
and tried again. You were willing to fail over and over and over,
and that is why you succeeded. How do I know this?
You are standing in front of me now."

I had tried, and I had failed. Now he was asking me to try again? What good would that do? I had already proven I couldn't do it.

But if I was honest, I wanted to believe I could.

So, even though I worried that I wasn't good enough, I decided to try again.

I worked and worked.

Then worked some more.

And while I could see it was a little better,
it still wasn't at all what I had wanted it to be.

I stormed up to the sculptor. "See? I told you I wasn't any good. And this proves it. Are you happy now?"

"Yes," he replied, "I'm happy.
It is good to see you sculpting."

"But it's terrible! I don't even know what
I'm making anymore."

"You're making progress," he explained. "I see talents emerging. I see risks being taken. I see courage. I see caring. I see perseverance. Yes, I see much progress, indeed. And I hope you will keep trying."

I tried again.

And again.

And again.

As I stepped back and looked at my work,
I had to admit, I wished I was better.

I went to talk to the sculptor, and he
asked me to go for a walk with him.

He said, "I know it can be hard when
things don't turn out as you had hoped,
but be proud of your failures. I know I am.
Every one of them."

"I can't imagine you ever failing."

He laughed. "More times than I can count.
But each time you fail, you get a little
smarter, a little braver, a little stronger.

"The truth is, we are all failures.
The dreamers, the doers, the creators...
Being a failure means you loved something.
You cared. It means you stepped forward,
you didn't hold back, you tried."

"That is why I brought you here."
He gestured to the statues around him.
"These are my friends. These are my failures.

"And I'm grateful for every one of
them because they helped me become
who I am today."

"I will tell you a secret," the sculptor confided.
"I am now much closer to the end of my life than
the beginning, and time passes whether we have the
courage to do something good and worthwhile,
or we don't."

It's been years since he's been gone.
I will always treasure the time I spent
with him. And I will never forget our
conversations or what he taught me:

"When we make it safe to fail,
we make it safe to succeed."

"How do I do that?"

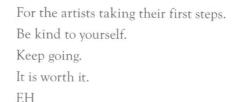

Dear Shale and Ever,
May you doubt your doubts,
challenge your challenges,
and dream your dreams.
Love,
Dad

For the artists taking their first steps.
Be kind to yourself.
Keep going.
It is worth it.
EH

COMPENDIUM.
live inspired

Written by: Kobi Yamada
Illustrated by: Elise Hurst
Edited by: Amelia Riedler
Art Directed by: Jessica Phoenix

Library of Congress Control Number: 2019957945 | ISBN: 978-1-970147-28-5

© 2021 by Compendium, Inc. All rights reserved. No part of this publication may be reproduced or transmitted in any form or by any means, electronic or mechanical, including photocopy, recording, or any storage and retrieval system now known or to be invented without written permission from the publisher. Contact: Compendium, Inc., 2815 Eastlake Avenue East, Suite 200, Seattle, WA 98102. *Trying*; Compendium; live inspired; and the format, design, layout, and coloring used in this book are trademarks and/or trade dress of Compendium, Inc. This book may be ordered directly from the publisher, but please try your local bookstore first. Call us at 800.91.IDEAS, or come see our full line of inspiring products at live-inspired.com.

2nd printing. Printed in China with soy and metallic inks on FSC®-Mix certified paper. A012011002

*Create
meaningful
moments
with gifts
that inspire.*

CONNECT WITH US
live-inspired.com | sayhello@compendiuminc.com

    @compendiumliveinspired
#compendiumliveinspired